W9-BLJ-965

DISCARD

Theodore and the Talking Mushroom

Theodore and the Talking Mushroom

Leo Lionni

Pantheon

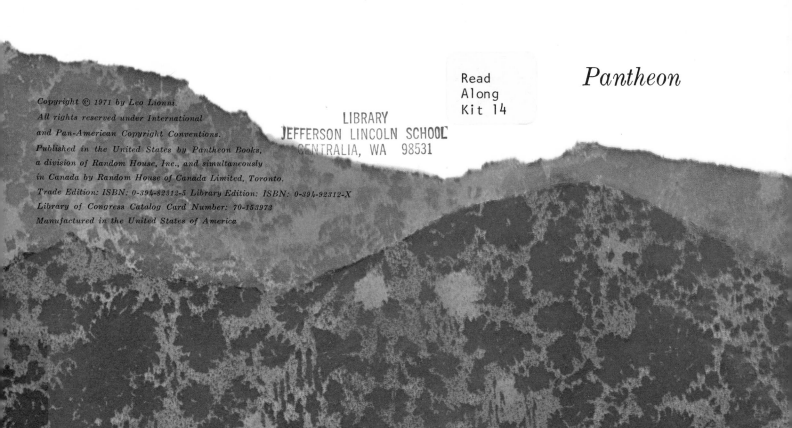

In the stump of an old oak there lived four friends — a lizard, a frog, a turtle, and a mouse called Theodore.

"Any time I lose my tail I can grow a new one," boasted the lizard.
"I can swim under water," said the frog.
"I can close like a box," said the turtle.
"And you?" they asked the mouse.
Theodore, who was always afraid, blushed. "I can run," he said.
The others laughed. "Ha! Ha! Ha!"

One day Theodore was frightened by a leaf that came fluttering down from a tree. "An owl!" he thought as he ran for cover.

Luckily he found a huge mushroom to hide under. He was too frightened to notice that it was as blue as an August sky. Theodore hid for a long time. He was tired. He had almost fallen asleep when suddenly . . .

. . . he was startled by a strange noise. "Quirp!"

Theodore looked around, his little heart beating wildly. But all was quiet. "I must have dreamed it," he thought, as he returned to the cool shade of the mushroom. He dozed off softly, when suddenly there was that noise again — "Quirp!"

It was the mushroom! Theodore was too excited to be frightened. "Can you talk?" he gasped. The mushroom did not answer, but after a little while it made the noise again. And again. Soon Theodore realized that the mushroom could not really speak. It could only say "Quirp."

Then he had an idea.

He went back to his friends. "I have something important to tell you," he said mysteriously. "Some time ago I discovered a talking mushroom. The only one in the whole world. It is the Mushroom of Truth and I have learned to understand its language."

He guided his friends toward the edge of the woods.

There stood the blue mushroom.

"Mushroom, speak!" Theodore commanded.

"Quirp!" said the mushroom.

"What does it mean?" asked Theodore's friends, dumbfounded.

"It means," said Theodore, "that the mouse should be venerated above all other animals."

The news of Theodore's discovery spread quickly.
His friends made him a crown.

Animals came from far away with garlands of flowers.

Theodore was no longer afraid. He did not have to run — he did not even have to walk. Wherever he went he was carried on the turtle's back on a cushion of flowers. And wherever he went he was venerated above all other animals.

One day he and his three friends went on a trip. They went
far beyond the edge of the woods through the fields of heather.
There lay the hills they had never crossed. The frog jumped ahead.
Suddenly, from the top of the hill, he shouted, "Look! Look!"

The valley below was filled with hundreds of blue mushrooms!
And a chorus of "**Quirps**" filled the air.

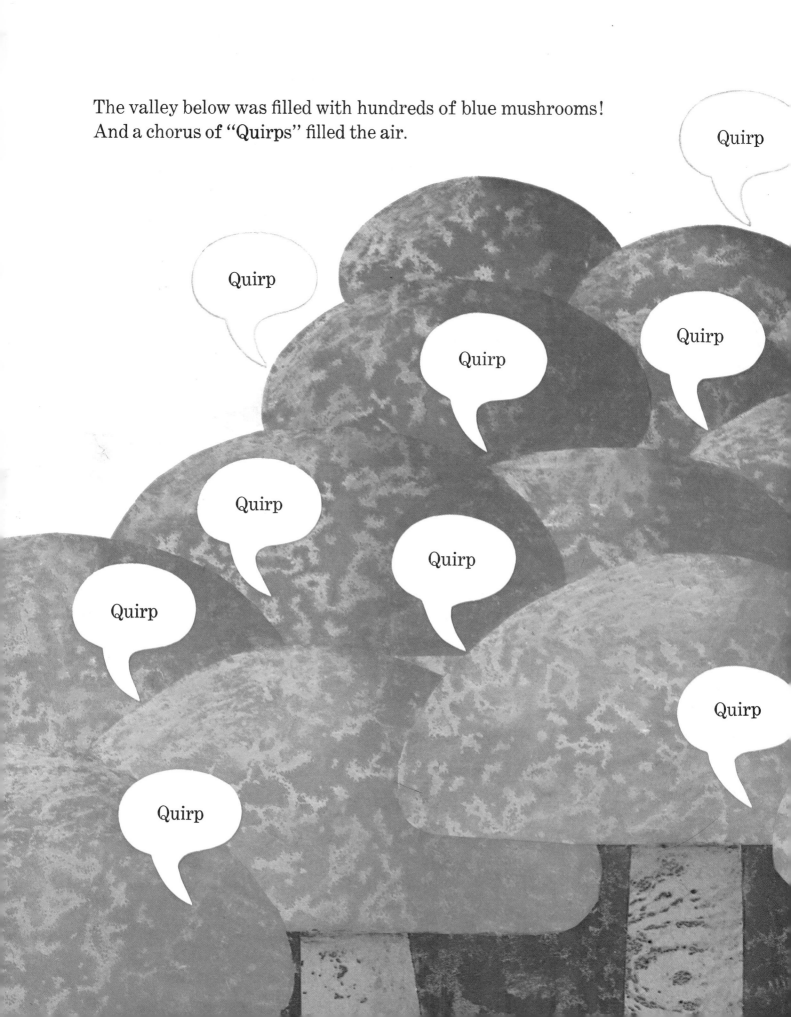

Speechless and bewildered they all gaped at the unexpected sight. Theodore knew he should say something but the words failed him and he just stood there trembling and stammering. Then his friends exploded with anger. "Liar!" "Faker!" "Fraud!" they shouted.

"Charlatan!" "Scoundrel!" "Impostor!"
    Theodore ran as he had never run before. Through the woods,
past the blue mushroom, past the old oak stump . . .

He ran and ran. And his friends never saw him again.

DATE DUE

FEB 23			
OCT 06			
MAR 24			
NOV 04			
FEB 28			